Pumpkins and Promises

The Halloween Collection Book 1

Dr. Hollaman

Copyright © [2023] by [Dr. Hollaman]

All rights reserved.

No portion of this book may be reproduced in any form without written permission from the publisher or author, except as permitted by U.S. copyright law.

Freebies

Join our newsletter mailing list today and we'll send you a free downloadable PDF and EPUB ebook right away. Then on the 1st of each month after that, we'll continue sending you a brand new free ebook. Sign up now to claim your first freebie and start receiving your monthly free ebooks!

Also, this book's free audiobook awaits! Allow your imagination to be whisked away by following along with the audiobook version, now accessible on our acclaimed Dr. Hollaman YouTube channel. Best of all, it's our audio gift to you! So sit back, relax those reading eyes, and let the melodic narration work its magic as you enjoy the fascinating tale in a new format. We sincerely thank you for joining us on this literary expedition and for making our publication dreams come true. Now go treat your ears to something good! The audiobook adventure begins now on YouTube, free for your listening pleasure. Happy reading...or should we say listening!

Contents

1

First Impressions

The October air was crisp on the morning Samantha stepped out into the pumpkin patch, inhaling the earthy scent of ripe gourds and fallen leaves. She crouched down to inspect the vines, plucking off a few stubborn weeds that had wormed their way between the large orange pumpkins. Most were ready for picking, their tough stems dried and withered.

Samantha stood, brushing the dirt from the knees of her jeans, and gazed out across the rolling fields surrounding her family's farm. The old red barn, paint faded and peeling, stood stalwart beside the sprawling farmhouse where she had lived her entire life. She knew every inch of this land, every hillock and furrow. It was achingly familiar.

She heard her father's voice calling from the barn, muffled but unmistakable. With a resigned sigh, Samantha headed toward the weathered structure, stepping into the dim interior. Shafts of dusty light filtered down from the loft above. Her father gave her a wave, then pointed toward a pallet loaded with crates.

"Morning, sunshine," he said, cheerful as ever. "Need you to haul those crates into the market for me. I've gotta run into town to pick up feed."

Samantha nodded, rolling up the sleeves of her flannel shirt and getting to work. It was the same routine, day after day. Wake with the sun, tend to the fields and the livestock. Keep the farm running smoothly. She didn't mind the labor, finding a simple pleasure in the repetition of farm life. But lately something seemed to be missing, a yearning she couldn't name.

As Samantha carefully stacked the last crate of gourds into the bed of the old pickup, she heard an engine rumbling up the gravel drive. An unfamiliar van rolled to a stop near the house, glossy and gleaming. Her brows knit together. They rarely got visitors all the way out here.

The van's door slid open and out stepped a man who looked as out of place as the vehicle itself. He wore dark jeans and a leather jacket. Aviator sunglasses perched atop his head of artfully tousled hair. Samantha crossed her arms, instantly wary. Just what she needed - a disruptive intruder.

"Howdy there!" the man said brightly, offering an exaggerated wave. "Name's Jack Colton. The town hired me to organize the Halloween festival this year. I'm told you provide the pumpkins?"

Samantha stiffened. So this was the big shot event coordinator she'd heard rumblings about, swooping in from the city to turn their modest festival into some kind of flashy production. She eyed him coolly.

"That's right," she said. "My family's been supplying the festival for over a decade. It's our honor to help celebrate our town's traditions."

"Excellent, excellent," Jack said, either oblivious to or choosing to ignore the edge in her voice. "Well, we're going to take things up a notch this year for sure. Hay rides, a haunted corn maze, food trucks - the works! And of course, we'll need lots and lots of pumpkins..."

As Jack prattled on about his elaborate plans, Samantha felt her jaw tightening. Did he think a few gimmicks could improve their humble harvest celebration? This was exactly what she'd feared when the town council announced they were bringing in an outside organizer.

"I'm sure we'll be able to provide a sufficient quantity of gourds," Samantha interjected, cutting Jack off mid-sentence. "Though we may need to discuss logistics, as I'll have to balance your request with our existing wholesale orders."

Jack spread his hands in an easy, conciliatory gesture. "Hey, I'm here to collaborate. We'll make sure this festival maintains the town's traditions while bringing in some new excitement too. Sound good?"

He flashed her a dazzling grin and, in spite of herself, Samantha felt her frostiness thawing ever so slightly. She gave a terse nod.

"I'll await your wholesale order then," she said briskly. "If you'll excuse me, I need to get to market. The pumpkins wait for no one."

Jack stepped back with a little mock bow. "By all means. We'll be in touch."

As Samantha climbed into the pickup and headed down the drive, she glanced back to see Jack standing with his hands on his hips, surveying the farm, no doubt envisioning the changes he wanted to make. Samantha frowned. Little did he know, she had no intention of letting him waltz in and upend generations of tradition. The battle lines were drawn. Game on.

2

Odd Couple

Over the next few weeks, Samantha felt like she was living in an alternate reality as Jack Colton fluttered around Pumpkin Creek making his grand plans. The normally sleepy town square was soon plastered with garish signs and flyers advertising things like "Jack's Spooktacular Spectacular."

Despite her best efforts to steer clear, Samantha soon found herself forced to meet with Jack frequently to coordinate pumpkin deliveries for the festival events. Each time, she gritted her teeth as he enthusiastically pitched concepts like pumpkin catapults and life-sized monster statues built from gourds.

"A little over-the-top, don't you think?" Samantha asked dryly after one of Jack's animated spiels about a pumpkin cannon show. "Next you'll suggest a flaming pumpkin fireworks display."

Jack laughed, a warm rumbling sound. "Hey, don't give me any ideas!" he said with a playful gleam in his eye.

Samantha had to fight to keep the corners of her mouth from turning up. She hated to admit it, but his enthusiasm was infectious. And working closely with him, she was starting to notice things - the way he drummed his fingers when thinking, how he tried to hide a yawn when they met early in the morning. It was...humanizing.

Still, they continued to clash on nearly everything. Jack insisted on taste testing every pumpkin dish being offered at the festival, while Samantha thought food trucks undermined local restaurants. Samantha wanted hayrides; Jack pushed for a haunted house.

"We're quite the odd couple, aren't we?" Jack remarked late one night as they pored over vendor contracts. He gave her a sideways smile. "But you know what they say - opposites attract."

Samantha's cheeks flushed at the implication. "Let's just focus on getting this festival planned, shall we?" she muttered, avoiding his gaze.

As the days passed in whirlwind of planning, Samantha found herself softening toward Jack more and more. Beneath his flashy exterior, she realized they shared a deep love of community and bringing people together. His passion was undeniable.

And if she were being fully honest, she enjoyed their lively debates and back-and-forth. He made her look at things in new ways, challenged her assumptions. It was...stimulating.

Samantha shook her head, clearing away such dangerous thoughts. She had a pumpkin farm to run, and the sooner this festival was over, the sooner she could get back to her normal routine. Alone.

The sound of laughter drew her attention, and she glanced over to see Jack cheerfully chatting with a group of children, letting them try on his aviator sunglasses. Okay, so maybe he wasn't all bad. In fact, she might even miss him a little bit once this was all over. But just a little.

3

Walls Come Down

Samantha sighed, pushing away the half-eaten plate of food. It was late, and she and Jack were once again the only ones left in the town hall as they finalized preparations for the festival's opening night.

"We still have to go over the schedules for hayride shifts and finishing carving those giant pumpkins for the stage set-up," she said wearily, taking a sip of lukewarm coffee.

Jack nodded, stifling a yawn. "Tell you what," he said, standing up and stretching. "How about we take a quick break first? Recharge our batteries. I saw a lovely little gazebo overlooking the lake just down the path. We could take a short walk."

Samantha hesitated. There was so much still to do...yet the thought of getting some fresh air was admittedly appealing. "I suppose a short break couldn't hurt," she conceded.

The night was mild, the air scented with woodsmoke. Jack gazed up at the starry sky as they strolled. "City lights drown all this out," he mused. "I'd almost forgotten how beautiful a really dark sky can be."

Samantha studied his profile, realizing how little she still knew about him. "What brought you out here anyway?" she asked. "You must have lived in some big cities before."

Jack nodded. "My dad's job had us moving all over when I was a kid - Atlanta, Chicago, Seattle. I learned to adapt, but it made me restless. I was always the new guy." He glanced over. "What about you? Have you always been here?"

"Born and raised," Samantha said with a wistful smile. "My family has owned the farm for generations. The thought of leaving terrifies me, to be honest. I like the predictability of my routines, the familiarity."

She paused, wondering why she was confessing such personal details. Somehow Jack's presence made her want to open up in ways she never had before.

They reached the gazebo, sitting on its weathered steps. Talking with Jack was easy, natural. The time slipped by until Samantha gave a reluctant sigh.

"I suppose we should head back," she said.

"Wait," Jack said, gently touching her wrist. His eyes were soft, face bathed in moonlight. Samantha's pulse quickened. Slowly, Jack leaned in close until his lips met hers in a gentle kiss.

For a moment, Samantha let herself get lost in the warmth of his embrace. As they finally broke apart, she exhaled shakily, any walls between them now crumbled and gone. Things would never be the same - she knew that much for certain. Whether that excited or terrified her, she couldn't yet say.

4

New Horizons

In the days after the kiss, Samantha threw herself into pumpkin harvesting and festival prep. If she kept busy, she didn't have to think about the fluttering in her chest whenever she pictured Jack's smile.

But avoiding him was impossible in a town as small as Pumpkin Creek. A week before the festival, Samantha bumped into Jack at the grocery store.

"Hey stranger," he said, eyes crinkling. "Haven't seen you around much."

Samantha tucked a strand of hair behind her ear self-consciously. "Just been busy getting everything ready."

An awkward silence stretched between them. Jack finally cleared his throat. "Well, I should let you get back to it. But first...maybe you'd like to take a drive with me this weekend? I'd love to show you this great lookout spot above the valley."

Samantha hesitated. A voice inside warned she was getting in too deep. But a larger part of her thrilled at the chance for adventure.

"I'd like that," she found herself saying. Jack's answering grin made her heart flutter all over again.

On Saturday evening, they drove winding roads to a remote ridge overlooking vibrant autumn foliage. The setting sun cast a golden glow over the vibrant landscape.

"It's beautiful up here," Samantha breathed, leaning on the viewpoint railing.

"Not as beautiful as you," Jack said. Before she could react, he pulled her into a passionate kiss. This time, she melted into his embrace without resistance, all her pent-up longing spilling over.

Under the starry sky, nestled in Jack's arms, the outside world seemed to melt away. Samantha felt light, free of her worries and inhibitions.

"You know what we should do?" she murmured later as they lay gazing up at the cosmos. "After the festival, we should get away - maybe a weekend trip to the city. I'd love for you to show me your world."

Jack propped himself up on one elbow, surprise mingling with delight. "I'd like nothing more," he said, leaning in to kiss her again.

Samantha sighed blissfully. With Jack, anything seemed possible. She was ready to venture beyond the familiarity of her farm and explore new horizons.

5

Growing Pains

Samantha took a deep breath as the train pulled into Chicago's bustling station. True to his word, Jack had planned a weekend getaway to show her his world. Though exhilarated, Samantha also felt unease creeping in. This glittering big city was so unlike her sleepy hometown.

Jack gave her hand a reassuring squeeze. "I can't wait to show you around," he said. "I think you're really going to love it here."

Despite Samantha's initial culture shock, soon she found herself enchanted by Chicago's energy and vibrancy. They strolled along the riverwalk, ate deep dish pizza, danced to a blues band at a lively club.

At a cocktail lounge overlooking the skyline, Samantha gazed out at the twinkling lights, nestled contentedly against Jack in their cozy booth. She felt giddy, lighter than air.

"I'm having an amazing time," she told Jack, smiling up at him. In the low light, he looked so handsome, it made her heart ache.

"Me too," Jack replied, kissing her tenderly. "These past few weeks with you have been incredible."

Samantha's pulse quickened at his words. "Do you really mean that?" she asked hesitantly.

Jack drew back, seeming to choose his next words carefully. "Of course I care about you," he said. "But you know I'm not one for commitment. My lifestyle has always been spontaneous, transient."

His voice was gentle, but Samantha felt like the ground had dropped out from under her. All her old insecurities came flooding back. She thought of her father, who had left when she was young. Of past boyfriends who had promised the world, then left without warning.

Blinking back tears, she shoved away from the table. "I should have known better," she choked out. "You'll get bored and move on just like every other man."

"Samantha, wait!" Jack called, but she had already rushed out of the lounge, lost in the crowds on the sidewalk. She had let her guard down, but now the fairy tale was over.

6

Crossroads

The bus ride back to Pumpkin Creek was miserable. Samantha alternated between resentment at Jack's words and berating herself for letting the weekend happen at all.

Back at the farm, she avoided her family's concerned questions and threw herself into harvesting. But she couldn't focus, her thoughts swirling endlessly.

Had she overreacted? Jack had seemed genuinely caring beneath his noncommittal words. And if she was honest, her own issues had contributed - the fear of abandonment she still carried.

But the thought of opening herself up again only to get hurt was terrifying. It would be so much easier to retreat to the safety of the farm, as she always had before.

As the festival opening grew closer, Samantha knew she had to make a choice. She could guard her heart and let Jack drift away. Or she could take a risk, confront her wounds, and try to salvage a future with him.

Her sleep was fitful that night. At one point, she dreamed she was standing at a crossroads beneath a full moon. Two paths diverged before her. One was bathed in sunlight and led to a vibrant garden.

The other was swathed in shadow, winding back through familiar fields.

When Samantha awoke, she knew what she had to do. Terrifying as it felt, for the first time, she was ready to walk away from the comfortable path. She had to find Jack. They had too much potential to just let it slip away without trying to heal the rift between them.

With renewed conviction, Samantha headed into town just days before the festival. She didn't know exactly what she would say, but she refused to hide from life's passions any longer. It was time to put her fears to rest once and for all.

7

Leap of Faith

Samantha paced nervously outside Jack's hotel as dusk fell over the town square. Candlelight glowed warmly in the windows as preparations continued for the festival's opening night.

Finally working up her courage, Samantha entered the lobby. The receptionist said Jack was upstairs overseeing the decorations in the ballroom, and gave her directions.

Taking a steadying breath, Samantha made her way up. The ballroom doors were propped open, and she could see Jack perched atop a ladder hanging bats and streamers from the ornate ceiling.

"It looks amazing in here," Samantha said tentatively.

Jack turned, eyes widening. He climbed down and approached her almost shyly.

"Samantha...I wasn't sure I'd see you before the festival," he said.

Samantha twisted her hands together anxiously. "I'm sorry for running off like that in Chicago," she said in a rush. "You didn't deserve it. The truth is, I was scared. But I don't want my issues to ruin this before it's barely started."

She met his gaze. "You make me feel alive in ways I've never known. I don't want to lose that. I'm willing to take a leap, if you still want to try..."

Her words were cut off as Jack swept her into his arms. "Of course I do," he murmured into her hair. "You don't know how much I've missed you."

Tension melting away, Samantha lost herself in their long-awaited kiss under the ballroom's glittering lights. With Jack, it felt like coming home.

Later, they walked hand in hand through the empty festival grounds. "It's perfect," Samantha sighed happily, picturing it filled with laughter and music come morning.

Jack smiled down at her. "This place brought me to you - I'll always be grateful for that."

Samantha's heart swelled. The future brimmed with promise and possibility. United, she knew they could weather any storms yet to come.

8

Blending Lives

Samantha awoke on festival morning with butterflies in her stomach. Today all their hard work would be put to the test.

She donned jeans and a casual flannel, then headed downtown. Jack stood on a ladder hanging the last of the pumpkin lights across Main Street as vendors set up booths along the sidewalks.

"It looks amazing!" Samantha called up to him. Jack grinned, climbing down to give her an excited kiss.

"This is going to be our best festival yet," he said, squeezing her hand.

As the day progressed, Samantha was amazed at how seamlessly she and Jack worked together attending to last minute tasks. While she ensured the pumpkin supplies were distributed and produce stands were well-stocked, Jack troubleshooted any issues with entertainment and vendors.

Seeing families, couples, and children streaming happily down the festival lanes warmed Samantha's heart. She realized this blending of her steadfast farm roots and Jack's lively urban vision perfectly captured the spirit of their community.

Dusk fell with carnival lights twinkling to life as a country band took the stage. Jack found Samantha by the apple bobbing station and drew her into an exuberant dance, the harvest moon beaming down on the celebration.

"I don't think Pumpkin Creek has ever seen a festival like this," Samantha marveled afterwards, slightly breathless as they walked hand-in-hand.

"We make a pretty great team," Jack agreed, giving her a quick spin that made her laugh.

With the festival underway, Samantha felt she and Jack had truly joined their once disparate worlds into one. Though the future remained uncertain, they would face it together - partners in both life and work.

9

Happy Endings

Music and laughter drifted through the brisk autumn air as the harvest festival continued late into the night. Families wandered the pumpkin patch hayrides, while couples swayed to the band in the town square.

Samantha stood backstage with Jack, surveying the festive atmosphere. "I can't believe it's almost over," she said wistfully.

Jack slid an arm around her waist. "I know, but we'll make the most of our last night." He gestures toward the band. "For instance, I believe I still owe you a dance."

Samantha smiled, allowing Jack to lead her into the square. Strings of lights twinkled above as they slow danced under the harvest moon. Samantha sighed contentedly, her head nestled against Jack's chest. She wished this moment could last forever.

Too soon, the music faded and they applauded the band's final song. "Come on, there's one more surprise," Jack said with a mysterious smile.

They walked hand in hand along a candlelit path to the pumpkin patch. In the moonlight, Jack had carved intricately detailed jack-o-lanterns depicting scenes from the festival's preparations.

Samantha gasped in delight, taking in each one. The carvings reminded her of everything they had weathered together these past weeks.

"It's wonderful," she breathed, turning to Jack with shining eyes. "I don't know how to thank you for this magical night."

"No need," Jack murmured, drawing her close. "You've given me so much happiness already."

As his lips met hers, Samantha was certain of one thing: together with Jack, she had found the happy ending she'd always dreamed of.

10

Ever After

Over the next few months, Samantha settled into a new normal, dividing her time between the pumpkin farm and frequent weekends visiting Jack in the city.

At first it was an adjustment, navigating the energetic crowds and bustling streets. But with Jack by her side, she grew to appreciate the vibrancy of urban life - the music, culture, and nightlife.

In turn, Jack made more trips to the countryside, helping Samantha around the farm and gaining an appreciation for the slower, simpler pleasures it offered. Their relationship grew deeper as they blended their once disparate worlds.

On a crisp December morning, Jack arrived to spend the holidays with Samantha's family. He pitched in harvesting the last pumpkins of the season, then joined her family around the fireplace that evening for hot cider and carols.

"I'm so happy you're here," Samantha whispered later, curled up with Jack under a down comforter.

"Me too," Jack murmured, kissing her forehead. "I know the long distance isn't always easy, but we'll make it work."

Samantha nodded, snuggling closer. The future was uncertain, but she knew their love could weather any storm. Just as seasons change, she mused, so too do people and relationships. She couldn't wait to experience all of life's adventures with Jack by her side.

The next morning, Samantha gazed out at the frost-covered fields glinting in the dawn light. The holidays had arrived, and a new year waited brightly on the horizon full of promise.

11

Full Circle

One year later

Samantha took a deep breath of crisp autumn air as she surveyed the town square, now decorated for another Halloween festival. She could hardly believe a whole year had passed since that fateful day when Jack first rolled into Pumpkin Creek.

So much had changed since then. Glancing down at the diamond ring on her finger, Samantha smiled. Just last week, Jack had proposed during a cozy dinner out on the farm. Of course she had excitedly said yes.

Strong arms slid around her from behind and Jack's familiar voice murmured "Good morning, fiancée" in her ear. Laughing, Samantha turned to give him a quick kiss.

"Can you believe the festival is already here again?" she marveled. "So much has happened since then."

Jack nodded, eyes full of warmth. "I'm so grateful this event brought us together. I can't imagine life without you now."

They spent the day strolling the festival hand in hand. Samantha was touched to see their collaborative pumpkin decorations from the previous year now displayed proudly around town.

That evening, they slow danced under the harvest moon just as they had a year ago. As the music swelled around them, Samantha laid her head contentedly on Jack's shoulder.

"I can't wait to do this every year for the rest of our lives," she whispered. No matter what new adventures life brought, she knew Jack would always be by her side.

In that moment, with their love stronger than ever, it felt like they had come full circle back to where their story began - but so much closer now.

The End

www.ingramcontent.com/pod-product-compliance
Lightning Source LLC
Chambersburg PA
CBHW071229140726
47996CB00004B/1534